The Day the
WORLD WAS
WEIGHED DOWN

Written by Chris Callaghan

Illustrated by Amit Tayal

Collins

Shinoy and the Chaos Crew

When Shinoy downloads the Chaos Crew app on his phone, a glitch in the system gives him the power to summon his TV heroes into his world.

With the team on board, Shinoy can figure out what dastardly plans the red-eyed S.N.A.I.R., a Super Nasty Artificial Intelligent Robot, has come up with, and save the day.

It was Monday morning, but Shinoy was having problems getting out of bed. He struggled to lift his head from the pillow. It felt *sooo* heavy.

"Just another five minutes," he thought. That would do it. But it didn't. His phone beeped and he saw a notification from the school library saying he had an overdue book. His mum was the school librarian! She could have just asked him.

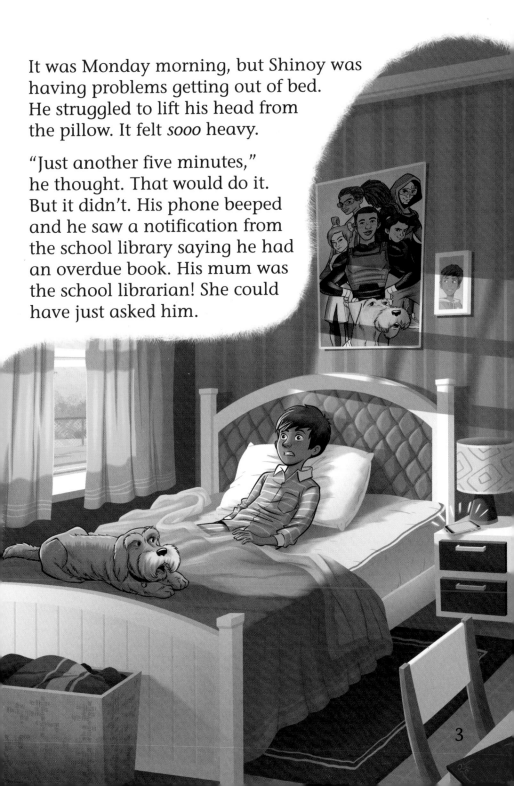

Shinoy managed to pull
open one of the curtains.
He hoped the light would help.
But it didn't. Everything was
such an effort. Slowly pulling
himself up on the windowsill, he
glanced outside.

A man was on all fours, c r a w l i n g
along the pavement. His dog, on the end of
a lead, was lying down. Birds swooped past
the window in strange rollercoaster patterns.
It was like they were too tired to fly upwards.
Even the trees looked saggy.

Shinoy's hand crept towards his phone. It was as heavy as a bar of gold and pulled him off the bed on to the floor.

There was only one thing to do. "Call to Action, Chaos Crew!" Usually, Shinoy loved to activate the special app on his phone with a dramatic movement. This time he only managed to lift his head slightly and press the app with the tip of his nose.

Merit appeared and instantly fell to his knees. "Ooof!" he muttered. "Not my most stylish entrance. What's going on, amigo?"

"You tell me!" Shinoy said, his voice muffled by the carpet.

"Could you get me a glass of water, please. I feel funny," Mum shouted from downstairs.

Merit did a slow commando crawl to the top of the stairs, with Shinoy dragging along behind.

"It's OK, Mum," Shinoy called. "The Chaos Crew is here."

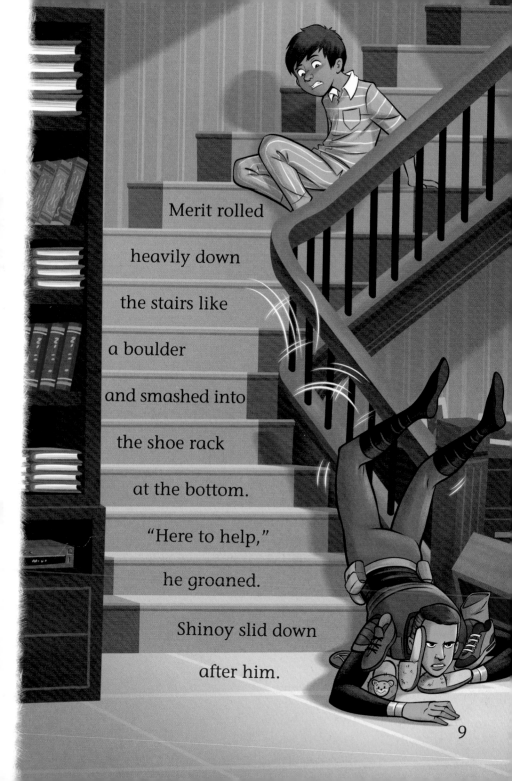

Merit rolled

heavily down

the stairs like

a boulder

and smashed into

the shoe rack

at the bottom.

"Here to help,"

he groaned.

Shinoy slid down

after him.

9

"It's mega-gravity," Merit said. "We have it on our world."

Shinoy remembered mega-gravity from series 3 when Merit left the universe. Suddenly, it made sense.

"It usually happens because there's a mega space-battle-cruiser in low orbit around a planet," Merit explained. "Are you at war with another world?"

"Not that I know of," said Shinoy.

Merit fiddled with his earpiece. "Is that you, Bug?" he said. "Great! Could you do an exosphere scan directly above my position, please, buddy?"

There was a pause.

"Roger that. I owe you a hot mocha with triple cream and marshmallows," said Merit.

Merit slowly lobbed a coin to Shinoy, which was hard to catch because of its weight. Shinoy couldn't believe what he was holding – a Chaos Crew Void Transit Disc.

"We're going into Space?" asked Shinoy.

Merit nodded. "Bug says there's a hunk of galactic grooviness dangling up there. It needs shifting." Then he shouted cheerfully to Shinoy's mum, "I'll have him back before school starts," as they fizzled out of sight.

When Merit and Shinoy refizzled, they were
in Space.

Once Shinoy had got over the shock of being on
a REAL spaceship, he had one important question.
"What if they steal our brains or something?"

"Don't believe everything you see on TV,"
laughed Merit. "Most beings in the universe are
pretty cool."

A polite voice said, "Borrowing or returning?"

They turned to see a lady sitting at a counter. Behind her were floors of books. They seemed to go on forever.

"Welcome to the Galactic Mobile Library Service," she said. "Are you borrowing or returning books?"

"Neither," said Merit. "We need to move your spacecraft to return the correct gravity to the planet below."

The librarian looked confused and checked her screen. "Somehow," she said, "we've crossed dimensions. That doesn't normally happen." She looked at Shinoy. "Our records show that you've got an overdue book."

Shinoy held up his phone. "Yeah, but I got a notification from the school library, not … this place!"

The librarian looked again at her screen. "Hmm. Yes. This overdue notice falls under the control of the Flat Hill school librarian, not the Galactic Mobile Library Service. A Doctor Snair has requested this book. That seems to have caused the error."

"I might have known," Shinoy sighed.

"Lucky for you, I'm an expert in crossing dimensions," Merit began, with a smooth smile at the librarian. "In fact, I'm the first human to leave the universe –"

Shinoy tugged on Merit's sleeve. "I've got to get back for school!"

"Ah yes. Well, in short, I need to move your super massive library out of Earth's orbit, in order to restore the correct gravity."

Merit turned to Shinoy. "You get back down there and I'll move this boat of books."

Shinoy took one last look around the spaceship and fizzled away.

In seconds, Shinoy was back on the sofa next to Mum.

Suddenly, the weight lifted from him. Merit must have flown the Galactic Mobile Library away! He ran upstairs and put his uniform on.

"Did you send a text about my overdue book?" he asked Mum.

"That's our new automated system," Mum said proudly. She paused. "You've got an overdue book? If you don't return them, what chance do I have of getting anyone else to?"

"Send out a spaceship to get them back?" Shinoy smiled.

"On my library budget? Although, what about ... library drones?"

Shinoy grabbed his overdue book, and laughed as he ran out. "OK, I'm returning it. Call off the drones!"

Library of the future

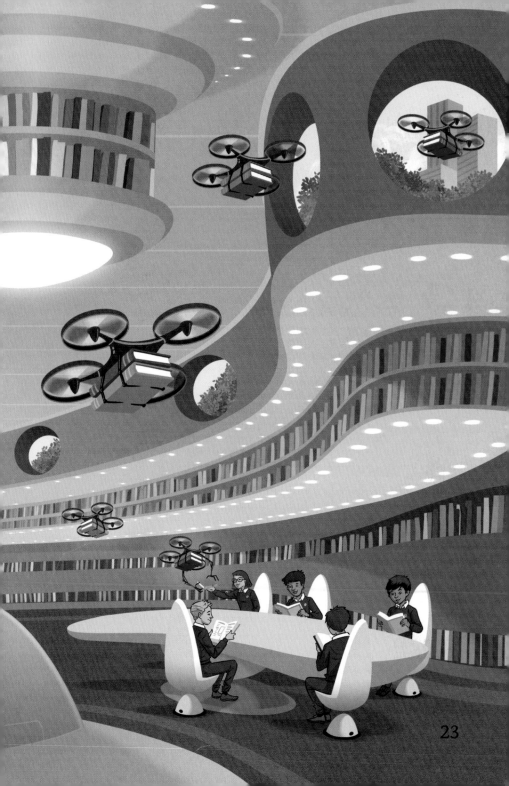

Ideas for reading

Written by Clare Dowdall, PhD
Lecturer and Primary Literacy Consultant

Reading objectives
- discuss the sequence of events in books and how items of information are related
- discuss and clarify the meanings of words, linking new meanings to known vocabulary
- discuss their favourite words and phrases
- answer and ask questions
- make inferences on the basis of what is being said and done

Spoken language objectives
- participate in discussions, presentations, performances and debates
- gain, maintain and monitor the interest of the listener(s)

Curriculum links: Science – Earth and Space; Forces

Word count: 970

Interest words: gravity, commando crawl, mega-gravity, universe, orbit, planet, exosphere, void, galactic grooviness, Galactic Mobile Library Service, dimensions

Resources: pencils and paper, grids for story planning, ICT for research

Build a context for reading
- Look at the front cover and read the title. Talk about the phrase 'weighed down', and ask if anyone knows what gravity is. Explain that gravity is a force that pulls things to the ground on earth. We are 'weighed down' by it.
- Read the blurb together and talk about what super-strength might do to the characters in the story.
- Check that children can read the interest words. Focus on the words acting as adjectives: *galactic* (relating to a galaxy) and *mega* (enormous). Check that children understand what they mean, and play with making new noun phrases, using them to describe environmental conditions, e.g. mega-heatwave, galactic snowstorm.

Understand and apply reading strategies
- Read pp2–5 to the children. Ask children to explain what is happening to Shinoy, reminding them that gravity is a force that pulls things to the ground.